BUGSLEY,
Where Are You?

PAGE PUBLISHING, INC.
Conneaut Lake, PA

First originally published by Page Publishing 2021

ISBN 978-1-6624-2157-0 (pbk)
ISBN 978-1-6624-2158-7 (digital)

Printed in the United States of America

BUGSLEY,
Where Are You?

Giovanna Ferrara

One day, two little sisters decided to go into the backyard to look for their puppy Bugsley.

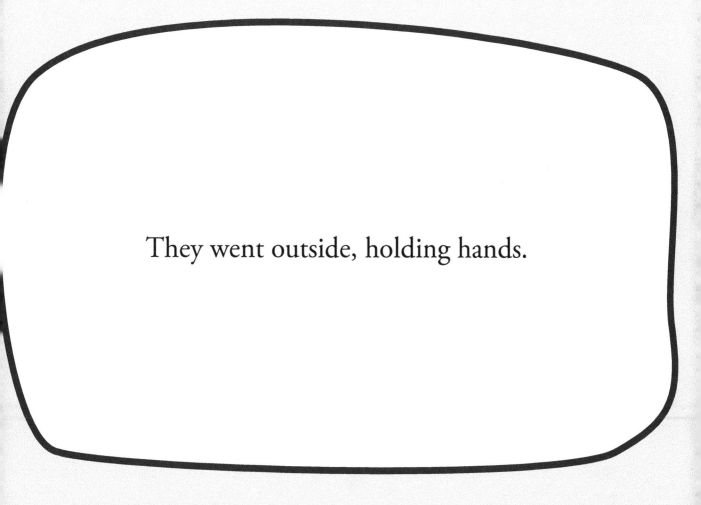

They went outside, holding hands.

"Let's look behind that tree," said
Gianna to her little sister.
"Yes," said Victoria.
"Let's look." They went behind the tree. "Bugsley!"
they both called out. "Are you here?"

No, Bugsley was not behind the tree. They were very disappointed. Bugsley was not behind the tree.

"Let's look behind the pool," said Gianna.
They both looked behind the pool.
Bugsley was not there.

"Oh my!" said Gianna, to Victoria.
Bugsley is not behind the pool.

"Bugsley, Bugsley, where are you?" they both yelled.
They couldn't find Bugsley.

13

"Where is he?" said Gianna.
"I don't know," said Victoria. "Let's
look behind the shed."

Still holding hands, the two sisters
went behind the shed.
"Bugsley, Bugsley, are you behind the shed?"
No, Bugsley was not behind the shed.
"Oh no!" cried Victoria. He's not behind the shed.

"I have an idea," said Gianna.
"Maybe he's inside the shed."

Gianna opened the shed door, and Bugsley was inside the shed sitting on the floor of the shed. He saw Gianna and Victoria. He got up and with his tail shaking. He was happy to see them.

"Bugsley, oh, Bugsley. We're so glad that we
found you," said both sisters in unison.
"Let's go home. Mommy is waiting for us."
For sure, as soon as the three of them walked
into the house, Mommy was so happy to
see them. She hugged them one by one.

About the Author

Giovanna Ferrara is a wife and mother of three grown children and four grandchildren.

Printed in the USA
CPSIA information can be obtained
at www.ICGtesting.com
LVHW072258281023
762291LV00007B/13